Mercy Watson: Something Wonky This Way Comes

Kate DiCamillo

Mercy Watson

Something Wonky This Way Comes

illustrated by Chris Van Dusen

CANDLEWICK PRESS

Text copyright © 2009 by Kate DiCamillo
Illustrations copyright © 2009 by Chris Van Dusen

First edition 2009

Library of Congress Cataloging-in-Publication Data is available.

Library of Congress Catalog Card Number 2009921688

ISBN 978-0-7636-3644-9

19 20 21 22 23 24 CCP 13 12 11 10 9 8

Printed in Shenzhen, Guangdong, China

This book was typeset in Mrs. Eaves.
The illustrations were done in gouache.

Candlewick Press
99 Dover Street
Somerville, Massachusetts 02144

visit us at www.candlewick.com

*For butter-eating, joy-seeking,
pig-loving readers everywhere*

K. D.

*To Kate DiCamillo,
who is truly a wonder*

C. V.

Chapter

1

Mr. Watson and Mrs. Watson have a pig named Mercy.

Mr. Watson, Mrs. Watson, and Mercy live together in a house at 54 Deckawoo Drive.

One Saturday afternoon, Mr. Watson said to Mrs. Watson, "My darling, my dear, there's a movie at the Bijou called *When Pigs Fly*."

"*When Pigs Fly!*" said Mrs. Watson. "What an inspiring title. Mercy, did you hear?"

Mercy did not hear.

Mercy did not hear because Mercy was not listening.

"It says here that the Bijou proudly serves real butter," said Mr. Watson.

"Oh, my," said Mrs. Watson, "real butter."

Mercy pricked up her ears.

She was listening now.

Mercy loved butter.

She particularly loved butter on
hot toast.

But she would take butter any way
she could get it.

"Yes," said Mr. Watson, "it says here that the Bijou proudly serves real butter on every Bottomless Bucket of popcorn."

"Bottomless?" said Mrs. Watson.

"Bottomless," said Mr. Watson, "which means 'all-you-can-eat.'"

"All-you-can-eat!" said Mrs. Watson. "What a delightful concept!"

Mercy thought that all-you-can-eat was a *very* delightful concept.

"Let's go to the movies!" said Mr. Watson.

"Let's!" said Mrs. Watson.

"Oink!" said Mercy.

Chapter 2

"Where are you going?" said Baby Lincoln.

"We're off to the movies!" said Mr. Watson.

"Oh," said Baby. "What movie are you going to see?"

"It is a movie called *When Pigs Fly*," said Mrs. Watson.

"Is it a romance?" said Baby. "Is it a movie about love?"

"Well," said Mrs. Watson, "I think it is basically a movie about pigs flying."

"Don't be ridiculous," said Eugenia Lincoln. "Pigs don't fly. It's a figure of speech."

"What's a figure of speech?" said Mr. Watson.

"The movie title," said Eugenia, "is a figure of speech signifying the impossible."

"Well," said Mrs. Watson, "we are going to be impossibly late if we don't get going."

"Would you care to join us?" said Mr. Watson.

"Yes!" said Baby Lincoln.

"Absolutely not," said Eugenia Lincoln.

"Oh, Sister," said Baby, "please say yes."

"No," said Eugenia.

But she got into the Watsons' convertible anyway.

"Where are you going?" shouted Stella.

"We're off to the movies!" said Mr. Watson.

"What kind of movie are you going to see?" said Frank.

"It's a romance," said Baby.

"It will be inspirational," said Mrs. Watson.

"It's a figure of speech!" shouted Eugenia.

"Is it a movie with a happy ending?" said Frank.

"Oh, it must end happily," said Mrs. Watson.

"Can we come, too?" said Stella.

"The more the merrier," said Mr. Watson.

Chapter 3

Police Officer Tomilello had the night off.

Officer Tomilello was at the Bijou Drive-In.

He was with his wife, Mrs. Officer Tomilello.

They were in the front row.

"Is it nice to have a night off from the relentless duties of keeping the world safe from crime?" Officer Tomilello asked himself.

"It is nice," he answered himself. "It is very nice."

Mrs. Officer Tomilello smiled.

Mrs. Officer Tomilello patted Officer Tomilello's arm.

Animal Control Officer Francine Poulet was at the Bijou Drive-In, too.

Animal Control Officer Francine Poulet was with Alfred P. Tomkins.

Alfred P. Tomkins and Francine
Poulet were on a date.

"Do you think that there will be actual pigs in this movie?" said Francine Poulet.

"I'm not certain," said Alfred P. Tomkins.

"As an Animal Control Officer," said Francine Poulet, "I have found pigs to be the wiliest clients of all."

"Really?" said Alfred.

"Absolutely," said Francine. "Although I did catch a pig once. At least, I *think* I caught a pig."

"Fascinating," said Alfred P. Tomkins, "simply fascinating."

He put his arm around Francine Poulet.

Chapter

4

Leroy Ninker was a small man with a big dream.

Leroy Ninker wanted to become a cowboy.

But for now, Leroy was working at the Bijou Drive-In concession stand.

Leroy Ninker was selling Bottomless Buckets of popcorn.

"Yippie-i-oh!" he shouted. "There's nothing faux! That's right. It's real butter, folks. Top-quality! Bottomless! And out of this world! Yippie-i-oh!"

In between pouring butter and popping popcorn, Leroy Ninker worked on his lasso skills.

He twirled the lasso.

He made the lasso whistle.

He lassoed a Bottomless Bucket.

He lassoed a stool.

"Yippie-i-oh!" sang Leroy. "There's nothing faux about my skill with a lasso."

Chapter
5

The Watson convertible pulled up to the Bijou ticket window.

"Help you?" said ticket seller Beatrice Leapaleoni.

"We are here to see *When Pigs Fly*!" said Mr. Watson.

Beatrice Leapaleoni took her glasses off.

She put her glasses back on.
She blinked.

"Um, pardon me and all," said Beatrice Leapaleoni, "but I'm seeing things kind of wonky. Is that a pig in the backseat of your vehicle?"

"Her name is Mercy," said Mr. Watson.

"She is our darling, our dear," said Mrs. Watson.

"I'm not sure pigs are allowed at the Bijou," said Beatrice Leapaleoni.

"Actually," said Mr. Watson, "she is a porcine wonder. Do you allow porcine wonders?"

"Porcine wonders?" said Beatrice Leapaleoni.

"Yes," said Mrs. Watson.

Beatrice Leapaleoni blinked.

"I don't think there are any rules against porcine wonders," she said.

"Excellent," said Mr. Watson. "Good evening to you, then."

Beatrice Leapaleoni blinked again. She adjusted her glasses.

"Wonky," said Beatrice Leapaleoni. "Wonky in the extreme."

Chapter
6

Mercy put her snout up in the air.

She sniffed.

There was a wonderful smell.

There was an incredible smell.

The wonderful, incredible smell was everywhere.

The wonderful, incredible smell was butter.

Mr. Watson said, "I think it's time for a Bottomless Bucket. Frank, why don't you and I go and get some treats for the ladies?"

At the concession stand, the little man behind the counter said, "Yippie-i-oh, what do you know?"

"Hey," said Mr. Watson, "you're the man who robbed us."

"Robbed you?" said Frank.

"Yes," said Mr. Watson. "He tried to take our toaster."

"My name is Leroy Ninker," said the little man.

"You're a thief," said Frank.

"Reformed," said Leroy Ninker.

"I'm a reformed thief studying to be
a cowboy."

"Well, good for you, Mr. Ninker,"
said Mr. Watson. "We would like several
Bottomless Buckets."

"Butter on those buckets?" said Leroy.

"We would like a great deal of butter on those buckets," said Mr. Watson.

"Yippie-i-oh," said Leroy, "that's the way to go."

Chapter
7

The smell of butter was absolutely everywhere.

The smell of butter was driving Mercy wild.

Where was the butter smell coming from?

Mercy thought she would go and investigate.

She leaped out of the convertible.

She moved with purpose.

Was there anything more heavenly than being hot on the trail of a true butter smell?

Mercy did not think so.

She trotted faster.

Mercy Watson was a pig on a mission.

Chapter
8

H ey, now," said Alfred P. Tomkins, "speaking of pigs, isn't that a pig right there?"

"Where?" said Francine Poulet.

"There," said Alfred P. Tomkins.

He pointed at the pig that was trotting past the truck.

The pig had its snout up in the air.

The pig looked very happy.

"That," said Francine Poulet, "is the pig from Deckawoo Drive. I have dealt with that pig before."

"I wonder what a pig is doing at the movies," said Alfred P. Tomkins.

"That's a good question," said Francine. "That's the kind of question that only an Animal Control Officer can answer."

"Fascinating," said Alfred P. Tomkins.

"Don't make any sudden movements," said Francine Poulet.

She reached into the back of her truck.

She grabbed her net.

"If you want to see an Animal Control Officer in action," said Francine Poulet, "follow me."

"Fascinating," said Alfred P. Tomkins, "simply fascinating. I'm right behind you."

Chapter
9

Mercy stopped.

She sniffed.

The smell of butter was very strong.

The smell of butter was very near.

The smell of butter was coming from
the backseat of a station wagon.

Mercy stuck her head in the window.
She sniffed again.

The smell of butter was coming from an extremely large bucket in the hands of a very small child.

Mercy helped herself.

The small child screamed. "Papa, Papa, a monster is eating my popcorn!"

Mercy chewed.

The popcorn was drenched in butter.

It was delicious.

A man stuck his face in Mercy's snout.

"What do you think you're doing?" the man said.

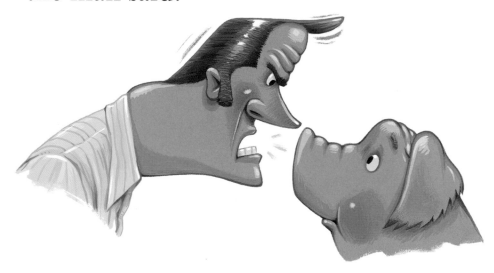

What did Mercy think she was doing?
She thought she was enjoying a buttery snack.

"Get out of there!" shouted the man.

He gave Mercy a very forceful shove.
Popcorn went flying everywhere.

Mercy thought that perhaps it was
time to move on.

Chapter
10

In the front row of the Bijou Drive-In, Officer Tomilello sat up straight in his seat.

Officer Tomilello said, "Did you hear that?"

Mrs. Officer Tomilello said nothing.

"Was that a scream of distress?" said Officer Tomilello.

"It sounded like a scream of distress," he answered himself.

"Is someone in trouble?" Officer Tomilello asked.

Mrs. Officer Tomilello said nothing.

"It is very possible that someone is in trouble," Officer Tomilello answered himself.

"Is it time for an officer of the law to step in?" Officer Tomilello asked.

"Most definitely," he answered.

Officer Tomilello put his badge around his neck.

He got his bullhorn from the backseat.

He kissed Mrs. Officer Tomilello good-bye.

He said, "Am I off to make the world a safer place?"

"I am," he answered himself. "I am most definitely off to make the world a safer place."

Mrs. Officer Tomilello waved good-bye.

Chapter
11

Mercy discovered that there was hot buttered popcorn everywhere.

Every car had big buckets of popcorn!

Every car had open windows!

The popcorn was buttery.

The popcorn was crunchy.

The popcorn was delicious.

Mercy helped herself.

She helped herself again.

And again.

People screamed.
People laughed.
People fainted.
Mercy kept eating.

In the meantime, Mr. Watson and Frank returned to the convertible with several Bottomless Buckets of popcorn.

Mrs. Watson was crying.

"My darling, my dear," said Mr. Watson, "what is wrong?"

"It's a tragedy," said Mrs. Watson.

"I wouldn't exactly call it a tragedy," said Eugenia Lincoln.

"Mercy is missing!" said Stella.

"Don't worry," said Mr. Watson. "We'll find her."

"I'll wait here, if you don't mind," said Eugenia Lincoln.

She helped herself to some hot buttered popcorn.

Chapter
12

Leroy Ninker heard people screaming about monsters.

Leroy Ninker heard people shouting about pigs.

Leroy Ninker saw a woman with a net run past the concession stand.

"What are you trying to catch?" said Leroy Ninker.

"A pig," said the woman with the net.

"A pig?" said Leroy Ninker.

"That's right," said the woman.

"You're not going to catch livestock with a net," said Leroy Ninker. "What you need is a lasso."

"Yippie-i-oh!"

Mr. Watson and Mrs. Watson and
Stella and Frank and Baby shouted,
"Mercy, Mercy, Mercy!"

"Should you remain calm?" Officer Tomilello asked. "You most definitely should remain calm."

At the ticket counter, Beatrice
Leapaleoni took her glasses off and
put them back on.

"Wonky," said Beatrice Leapaleoni.
"Wonky in the extreme. Maybe it's
some kind of emergency. Maybe I
should call for help."

Beatrice Leapaleoni adjusted her glasses.

She picked up the phone.

Beatrice Leapaleoni dialed the fire department.

Chapter
13

Mercy was having a wonderful time.

She had consumed a large amount of buttered popcorn, and now people were chasing after her.

Mercy loved a chase.

She ran faster.

She kicked up her heels.

"Gotcha!" shouted Francine Poulet.
Francine Poulet netted Officer
Tomilello.

"Yippie-i-oh!" shouted Leroy Ninker.
He lassoed Francine Poulet.

"Fascinating," said Alfred P. Tomkins,
"simply fascinating."

There was the sound
of a siren. There was the
flash of lights.
  A fire truck pulled
into the Bijou.

"Things seem to be out of control,"
said the fireman named Ned.

"It's the movies," said the fireman
named Lorenzo. "They make people
crazy."

"Actually," said a man who was standing next to Ned, "I think the pig is making people crazy."

"Holy smokes, I know that pig!" said Lorenzo. "It's that toast-loving pig from Deckawoo Drive."

"I'll tell you," said the man standing next to Ned, "this is way better than any movie I've ever seen. It's all been fascinating, simply fascinating."

"I guess it's time for us to come to the rescue," said Ned.

"We should do what only firemen
can do," said Lorenzo.

Ned and Lorenzo took off running.

Ned and Lorenzo ran very fast.

Ned and Lorenzo caught up with Mercy.

"Hey," said Ned, "how's about some toast?"

"Yes," said Lorenzo, "how's about some toast with a great deal of butter?"

Mercy stopped running.

Mercy sat down.

Mercy thought very hard.

Toast sounded like an excellent idea to her.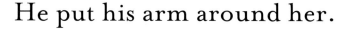

Toast *always* sounded like an excellent idea to her.

Ned sat down next to Mercy.

He put his arm around her.

"Oh," said Mrs. Watson, "you found her!"

"How will we ever be able to thank you for helping us locate our darling, our dear?" said Mr. Watson.

"Well," said Ned, "I'm a little hungry."

"Toast would be good," said Lorenzo.

"Toast," said Mrs. Watson. "I would love to make some toast. Who else would like some toast?"

"We never did get to see that movie," said Stella.

"I wonder if it ended happily," said Frank.

"Well," said Mrs. Watson, "here we are, all of us together."

"And we're all eating toast," said Mr. Watson.

"I can't imagine a happier ending than that," said Mrs. Watson.

"It's the happiest possible ending," said Baby Lincoln. "It's almost like a love story."

"It *is* a love story," said Mr. Watson.

"And it's very inspirational," said Mrs. Watson.

Join MERCY WATSON in all six of her pig tales!

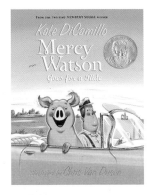

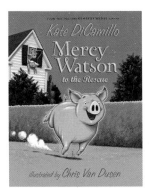

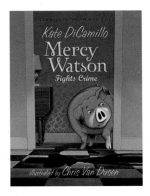

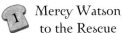 Mercy Watson
to the Rescue

2 Mercy Watson
Goes for a Ride

3 Mercy Watson
Fights Crime

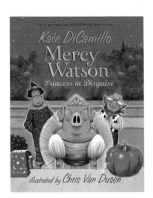

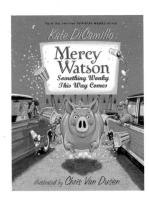

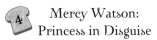 Mercy Watson:
Princess in Disguise

5 Mercy Watson
Thinks Like a Pig

6 Mercy Watson:
Something Wonky
This Way Comes

Kate DiCamillo is the renowned author of numerous books, including *The Tale of Despereaux* and *Flora & Ulysses*, both of which won the Newbery Medal. After writing *Mercy Watson: Something Wonky This Way Comes*, she said, "This is the last Mercy Watson book. I hate writing those words. I hate writing them so much that I might have to write another Mercy Watson book just to cheer myself up. So, don't go away just yet. Working with a pig (and Chris Van Dusen) has taught me that anything is possible." Five years later, the first book in the spin-off series, Tales from Deckawoo Drive, was published, and four years after that, a picture book origin story, *A Piglet Named Mercy*, followed. Kate DiCamillo lives in Minnesota.

Chris Van Dusen is the author-illustrator of *Down to the Sea with Mr. Magee, A Camping Spree with Mr. Magee, The Circus Ship, King Hugo's Huge Ego, Hattie & Hudson,* and *Randy Riley's Really Big Hit*. He says, "Illustrating the Mercy Watson books has been an absolute joy! I'd like to thank Ann Stott for sending Mercy trotting my way. Thanks also to Karen Lotz for all of your support and to Pam Consolazio, who patiently watched my deadlines come and go. Finally, I am forever indebted to Kate for trusting me with her wonderful words. Thank you for the colorful characters, wonky adventures, and all the laughs along the way." Chris Van Dusen has continued to draw Mercy and her neighbors in the spin-off series, Tales from Deckawoo Drive, and a picture book origin story, *A Piglet Named Mercy*. He lives in Maine.

Navigate a neighborhood full of mishaps,
mayhem, and a lot of hot buttered toast.

Tales from Deckawoo Drive